UNDER the RAINBOW

G. B. Queen

ISBN 978-1-953223-19-7 (paperback)
ISBN 978-1-953223-15-9 (digital)

Rev. date: 04/23/2021

Rushmore Press LLC
1 800 460 9188
www.rushmorepress.com

Printed in the United States of America

Her hair waved in the warm ocean spray after she stared at the birds close by and looked away. On a warm summer day on the Atlantic Ocean, a little girl named Rainbow Starkid boarded a fishing boat to search for big tuna. Her face was pink and had a smile of joy on it. She stared into the water to see a bright yellow sunbeam flicker from orange to white. She took a deep breath in surprise and felt excited about spending a few days on the boat with her parents. She enjoyed being in water. Adventures on the water allowed her to have fun and enjoy nature.

At eight o'clock in the morning, Rainbow joined her parents at the dining area for a morning meal. She sat at the table next to her mom and watched her dad, Captain Starkid handle the food. She poured milk into everyone's glasses and requested grits, scrambled eggs, and hash browns with turkey bacon as her breakfast items. She gave her mom half of her turkey bacon and hash browns for four green apple slices. When all of the food was eaten, she asked her parents if she could take a quick swim before the fishing contest started. After a brief discussion, Rainbow changed into her pink and black wet suit, fins, and snorkel gear.

With permission to use the diving board, Rainbow leaped high into the air and dove into the sparkling blue water. She grinned after she gasped for air and felt the warm water splash onto her chin and cheeks.

In the water, she saw many shiny reflections and brilliant colors. She was surprised to see kinds of fish that she had never seen before. She swam toward the ocean floor and saw purple and pink polka-dotted fish, yellow glowing fish, and blue dolphins.

At the bottom, Rainbow felt cold water stiffen her legs. She watched the strange fish move in and out of a trail of bubbles. She paused and felt like she had taken a deep breath. She touched the sand on the ocean floor and glanced up to the top to see a white beam of light pass through the bubbles. On the way to the top, she discovered something human-like that had a large sparkly yellow tail and purple fin. Her first thought was to quickly return to the boat to tell her parents all about the strange creature.

Back on deck, Rainbow shouted about the strange creature until her voice became hoarse. She told her dad, but she had no idea how to make him believe the story. She glanced over the side of the boat and told her mom about its beautiful pink hair. After she told them about its big shiny tail and matching top, she watched them glance at each other and smile. Rainbow felt like her parents were not listening to her, and she thought that maybe it was because of her brilliant imagination.

At 10:00 am, Rainbow smelled the saltwater in the air. From the corner of her eye, she saw seagulls dive into the water and come out with fish dangling in their mouths. She turned around to see fish leaping out of the water and into the air. She wondered why the birds were swimming, and fish were trying to fly beside the boat.

Rainbow heard her dad say that the fish and the birds wanted different things. She wondered why the creatures wanted different things and decided to search for her mom to ask more questions. Rainbow wished that she could be like the beautiful fish, but she was born as a beautiful little human girl with two legs and ten toes.

Rainbow ran down the stairs of the main deck and stood at the master cabin room door. She yelled her questions to her mom. Immediately, she heard her mom say that the birds wanted food, and the fish wanted schools to keep away from sharks. Afterwards, Rainbow understood the idea and ran back to the main deck to watch her dad participate in the fishing contest.

Outside, Rainbow crawled to the edge of the deck and peered into the water. She watched her dad reel in a big barracuda that had green spots and gray stripes. She stood up and saw the fish fight and splash water in every direction. Rainbow looked up, down, left, and right before she turned to see her dad slide across the deck. She heard loud squeaks come from his boots and glanced down into the water to see the big barracuda escape her dad's fishing line.

After Rainbow watched the barracuda disappear, she wandered to her favorite spot at the other end of the boat and sang her favorite song. She grabbed the rail and leaned over the edge to see a strange pair of eyes glisten in the water. She paused in silence and thought she was seeing her own reflection. She admired how they seemed to change colors and glow. She raised her hand and saw the creature raise its hand and wave.

Rainbow watched the strange creature pop up out of the water and smile. She felt a warm breeze and watched the water bead off of the strange creature's long pinkish-orange wavy hair. She blinked and watched the creature vanish. Her eyes were open and stuck in amazement. She jumped into the water to greet the mysterious creature, but it was nowhere to be seen.

At 12:12pm, Rainbow met her parents at the dining area for lunch. She had honey baked ham, chicken, kale chips, apple sauce, and a large glass of lemonade. The minute that Rainbow became full, she stretched her arms across the table, looked back at the clock on the wall and smiled. She was exhausted from singing and watching for the mysterious creature to reappear. In the back of her mind, she could only imagine why it was so shy.

Down below deck in Rainbow's cabin room, she sat in bed and thought to make a note in her diary. Before she drifted to sleep, she looked at her diary and wrote. "Something was in the water. I wish that I could swim in the water without needing any air. My parents seem to think that I am using my imagination to come up with the idea of seeing a human-looking fish. It appears to be a girl, but I want to know what she wants. She likes my voice and seems to be very nice and friendly. Before the weekend is over, I will find this fish and convince it to come back to the boat for my mom and dad to see. They say there is nothing real about mermaids."

Rainbow fell into a deep sleep with her pencil placed on the inside of the day's diary page. In her dream, Rainbow saw her dad fishing on the boat and a mermaid in the water below. She yelled that the mermaid would get tangled in the fishing line, but she didn't hear any reply. In her mind, her dad couldn't hear and might only see a tuna fish. She looked at its beautiful pinkish orange hair and began to sing. Rainbow paused and placed her hand behind her ear. Rainbow heard the mermaid repeat every sound as if there was an echo. The more Rainbow sang to the mermaid, the closer she could study its swim style. She saw how happy the mermaid became and sang to it in a softer voice.

Rainbow heard the mermaid say that she wanted to be friends. She listened to her talk about currents in the water and her favorite colors. She agreed to share stories about what she saw on land and how to live in and out of the water. She learned about swimming parallel to escape rip currents and other lessons about water safety.

Not too far from the boat, Rainbow looked back to see the mermaid swim away and followed the trail of bubbles coming from behind its tail. She was curious when the bubbles disappeared into a cave.

At the center of the cave, Rainbow found the mermaid laying in a large seashell. She laid onto the sand and told the mermaid her questions. She popped up in excitement after she heard the mermaid answer all of her questions. Rainbow's most important question was her wish.

Rainbow saw three colorful shadows appear from inside the cave. She was amazed to see the shadows grow larger and larger right before her eyes. She looked into the mermaid's eyes and found trust. She watched the mermaid swim up and glance back at the large seashell.

The next thing that Rainbow saw was magnificent. She turned to the side to see a treasure chest appear from behind a sparkly haze of dust. She watched it open, and to her surprise, she found a crystal-studded tail. Her wish to swim with no air was answered. She glanced up to see three beautifully styled sister mermaids staring back at her.

Rainbow screamed in delight and fanned her tail in the water as if it was a ceiling fan. Round and round, she followed after her mermaid friend and three mermaid sisters and played hide-and-seek around the cave. After finding the smaller mermaid sister, Rainbow followed the other mermaid sisters into the lower part of the cave. Rainbow swam so fast that she found the dark end of the water. The water became too dark and the gam became too much fun. In a blink of an eye, Rainbow didn't see any of her mermaid friends. She thought to tell them about the plan for meeting up later but thought they were too far gone to hear her voice.

Rainbow blinked and awoke in her cabin room with her arms around her pillow. She wanted to find the next adventure. In her mind, she pictured the extraordinary cool colors of the mermaids' hair and nails. She jumped out of bed and ran to the window. She was expecting to see all of the beautiful mermaids, but none were in sight.

She went to the master cabin room, but her mom was not there. After looking everywhere on the lower deck of the boat, Rainbow frowned half-way up the stairs. She felt like everybody left her behind and sung a song.

Rainbow stood near the top of the stairs and heard lots of loud boat engines in the distance. She glanced up into the sky to see a vibrant rainbow appear in front of a patch of clouds. She turned her head to find her parents leaned over the side of the boat. Just in case she was still dreaming, Rainbow told her mom and dad about her lovely nap and dream. She saw them roll their eyes, shake their heads, and make silly faces. After a short period of silence, Rainbow closed her eyes and hummed her favorite calypso melody. She dropped to her knees when she saw the friendly mermaid, and three small heads of hair popped out of the water. She finally had a dream and wish come true.

The End

9 781953 223197